## DOG BREEDS

# BLOODHOUNDS

BY SHANNON JADE

# WWW.APEXEDITIONS.COM

Copyright © 2025 by Apex Editions, Mendota Heights, MN 55120. All rights reserved. No part of this book may be reproduced or utilized in any form or by any means without written permission from the publisher.

Apex is distributed by North Star Editions:
sales@northstareditions.com | 888-417-0195

Produced for Apex by Red Line Editorial.

Photographs ©: Shutterstock Images, cover, 1, 6–7, 15, 16–17, 18, 20–21, 22–23, 25, 26–27, 29; Kim Raff/The News & Advance/AP Images, 4–5; H. Rick Bamman/Northwest Herald/AP Images, 9; iStockphoto, 10–11, 12–13, 14, 24

**Library of Congress Control Number: 2023921623**

**ISBN**
978-1-63738-904-1 (hardcover)
978-1-63738-944-7 (paperback)
979-8-89250-041-8 (ebook pdf)
979-8-89250-002-9 (hosted ebook)

Printed in the United States of America
Mankato, MN
082024

## NOTE TO PARENTS AND EDUCATORS

Apex books are designed to build literacy skills in striving readers. Exciting, high-interest content attracts and holds readers' attention. The text is carefully leveled to allow students to achieve success quickly. Additional features, such as bolded glossary words for difficult terms, help build comprehension.

# TABLE OF CONTENTS

**CHAPTER 1**
SEARCH AND RESCUE  4

**CHAPTER 2**
THEN AND NOW  10

**CHAPTER 3**
BLOODHOUND BASICS  16

**CHAPTER 4**
CARE AND TRAINING  22

COMPREHENSION QUESTIONS • 28
GLOSSARY • 30
TO LEARN MORE • 31
ABOUT THE AUTHOR • 31
INDEX • 32

CHAPTER 1

# SEARCH AND RESCUE

A bloodhound searches for a lost girl. The dog smells the girl's jacket. Then he sniffs the air.

Bloodhounds often work as search dogs. They find people who have gone missing.

Bloodhounds can follow smells in the air or on the ground.

The dog picks up the girl's scent. He tracks her trail through the woods. A search and rescue team follows him.

### SUPER SMELLING
A bloodhound's sense of smell is about 1,000 times better than a human's. Bloodhounds can follow very faint scents. They can smell trails that are 12 days old.

The bloodhound walks and sniffs for hours. At last, he finds the girl. The dog barks to **alert** his team. They bring the girl home.

FAST FACT

Bloodhounds can follow a trail for more than 130 miles (209 km).

Search dogs go through years of training. They learn how to find people in many places.

CHAPTER 2

# THEN AND NOW

**B**loodhounds have their **origins** in **medieval** Europe. People there bred scent-hunting hounds. These dogs helped hunt animals and track people.

People were breeding bloodhound-like dogs in France in the 600s CE.

By the 1300s, people in England were calling the dogs bloodhounds. The dogs had black-and-tan fur. By the 1800s, the **breed** had spread to the United States.

People often owned many bloodhounds. The dogs hunted in packs.

**FAST FACT**
Early bloodhounds helped people hunt deer and boars.

Many bloodhounds were working dogs. Some tracked animals. Others helped catch **criminals**. Bloodhounds still do these jobs today. They are also popular pets.

Police officers have used bloodhounds for hundreds of years.

Bloodhounds can learn many tricks and tasks.

## FIGHTING CRIME

Bloodhounds often work with the police. Some dogs find missing people. Others search for **suspects**. Their work can help solve cases.

CHAPTER 3

# BLOODHOUND BASICS

Bloodhounds are big dogs. Full-grown bloodhounds weigh up to 110 pounds (50 kg). They stand about 25 inches (64 cm) tall at the shoulder.

Bloodhounds have long legs. They are fast runners.

Bloodhounds have loose skin with deep folds. Their heads and necks are especially wrinkly.

**FAST FACT**

Because of their loose skin, bloodhounds drool a lot. They may leave puddles.

◀ Bloodhounds tend to drool more when they're excited.

Bloodhounds have a better sense of smell than any other dog.

A bloodhound's fur is short and thick. It can be black, tan, or red. The dogs also have very long ears.

## STIRRING UP SCENTS

A bloodhound's long ears help it track scents. The ears drag on the ground as the dog walks. They stir up smells into the dog's nose.

CHAPTER 4

# CARE AND TRAINING

**B**loodhounds need to be brushed every week. Owners should also clean the folds in the dogs' skin and ears. That way, the skin won't get hurt or **infected**.

A bloodhound's long ears can easily pick up dirt and germs.

**Owners should take their bloodhounds on walks every day.**

Bloodhounds were bred to work. So, they are very active dogs. Most bloodhounds need at least two hours of exercise every day.

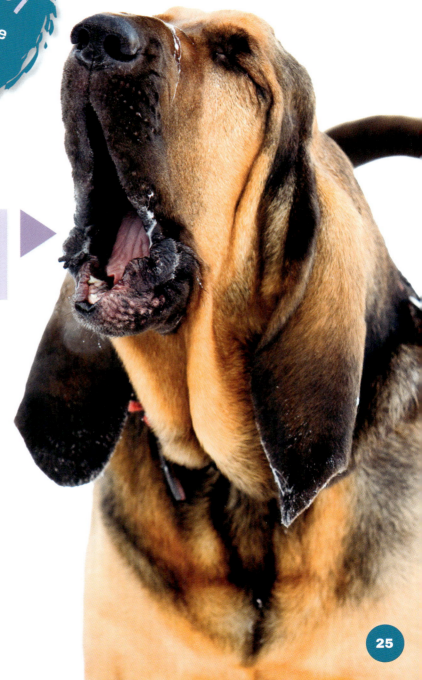

**FAST FACT**
Bloodhounds are vocal dogs. They howl or bay.

Bloodhounds may bay when they're lonely or when they pick up a smell.

Training is important, too. Bloodhounds are smart. But they can be **stubborn**. They may not listen, especially when following a scent. Owners should be patient and **consistent**.

## GENTLE GIANTS
Even though bloodhounds are large dogs, they tend to be gentle. Bloodhounds are calm and sweet with people, especially their owners. They often get along well with other animals.

People should start training bloodhounds when the dogs are puppies.

# COMPREHENSION QUESTIONS

*Write your answers on a separate piece of paper.*

1. Write a sentence describing one way owners should care for bloodhounds.

2. Would you like to have a bloodhound as a pet? Why or why not?

3. How much do bloodhounds weigh?
    - A. less than 12 pounds (5 kg)
    - B. up to 110 pounds (50 kg)
    - C. more than 130 pounds (59 kg)

4. How would stirring up scents help a bloodhound follow a trail?
    - A. More smells would stay under the ground.
    - B. All smells would be sent farther away from the dog.
    - C. The right smell would be more likely to reach the dog's nose.

**5.** What does **wrinkly** mean in this book?

*Bloodhounds have loose skin with deep folds. Their heads and necks are especially wrinkly.*

- **A.** full of lines and ridges
- **B.** very thin and light
- **C.** made of plastic

**6.** What does **gentle** mean in this book?

*Even though bloodhounds are large dogs, they tend to be gentle. Bloodhounds are calm and sweet with people, especially their owners.*

- **A.** kind
- **B.** loud
- **C.** angry

Answer key on page 32.

# GLOSSARY

**alert**
To let someone know something is happening.

**breed**
A specific type of dog that has its own looks and abilities.

**consistent**
Done the same way over and over.

**criminals**
People who break laws.

**infected**
Filled with germs, which cause pain and other problems.

**medieval**
Related to a period of history that lasted from about 500 CE to about 1500 CE.

**origins**
The early parts of something's history.

**stubborn**
Not willing to change how one thinks or acts.

**suspects**
People the police think may be guilty of a crime.

# To Learn More

## BOOKS

Green, Sara. *Hounds*. Minneapolis: Bellwether Media, 2021.

Lilley, Matt. *Search and Rescue Dogs*. Mendota Heights, MN: Apex Editions, 2023.

Pearson, Marie. *Dogs*. Mankato, MN: The Child's World, 2020.

## ONLINE RESOURCES

Visit **www.apexeditions.com** to find links and resources related to this title.

## ABOUT THE AUTHOR

Shannon Jade writes both fiction and nonfiction books. She lives in Australia alongside some of the world's greatest landscapes and most amazing animals.

# INDEX

**A**
alert, 8

**B**
breed, 12

**C**
consistent, 26
criminals, 14

**E**
ears, 20–21, 22
England, 12

**I**
infected, 22

**M**
medieval, 10

**O**
origins, 10

**S**
search, 4, 7, 15
smell, 4, 7, 21
stubborn, 26
suspects, 15

**T**
track, 7, 10, 14, 21

**U**
United States, 12

**W**
working, 14–15, 24

**ANSWER KEY:**
1. Answers will vary; 2. Answers will vary; 3. B; 4. C; 5. A; 6. A